D0708411

Rainforest Explorer

By Rupert Matthews

LONDON, NEW YORK, MUNICH,
MELBOURNE, AND DELHI

DK LONDON
Series Editor Deborah Lock
Project Art Editor Hoa Luc
Producers, Pre-production
Francesca Wardell, Vikki Nousiainen

Reading Consultant
Shirley Bickler

DK DELHI
Editor Pomona Zaheer
Assistant Art Editor Yamini Panwar
DTP Designer Anita Yadav
Picture Researcher Surya Sarangi
Dy. Managing Editor Soma B. Chowdhury

First published in Great Britain by
Dorling Kindersley Limited
80 Strand, London, WC2R 0RL

Copyright © 2014 Dorling Kindersley Limited
A Penguin Random House Company
10 9 8 7 6 5 4 3 2 1
001—253406—June/2014

A CIP catalogue record for this book is available
from the British Library.

ISBN: 978-1-40935-191-7

Printed and bound in China by South China Printing Company.

The publisher would like to thank the following for
their kind permission to reproduce their photographs:
(Key: a-above; b-below/bottom; c-centre; f-far; l-left; r-right; t-top)

1 Dreamstime.com: Patryk Kosmider. 6 Alamy Images: Jeremy Sutton-Hibbert (t). 7 Corbis: Wolfgang Kaehler (b).
10 Alamy Images: GM Photo Images (c). 11 Alamy Images: Sue Cunningham/Worldwide Picture Library (t).
12 Alamy Images: Realimage (crb); Andrew Twort (cr). 13 Alamy Images: Andrew Paterson (crb); Studiomode (tr);
ImageDB/PhotosIndia.com LLC (cr). Dreamstime.com: Jo Ann Snover (br). 17 Corbis: Susanne Borges/A.B. (c).
18 Corbis: Konrad Wothe/Minden Pictures (c). 19 Alamy Images: Morley Read (t). 23 Dorling Kindersley: Laszlo
Veres. 25 Corbis: Jeffrey Bosdet/All Canada Photos (c). 26 Corbis: Top Photo Group (t). 27 Corbis: Gordon Wiltsie/
National Geographic Society (b). 29 Alamy Images: Nigel Hicks (c). 30 Corbis: Sung-IL Kim/Sung-Il Kim (t).
31 Dorling Kindersley: Rough Guides (ca). 33 Corbis: Kevin Schafer (cb). 34 Dorling Kindersley: Thomas Marent (c, bc).
36 Corbis: W. Perry Conway (crb); Kevin Schafer (cra). 37 Corbis: Michael & Patricia Fogden (cla, cra); Kevin Schafer
(clb, crb). 41 Alamy Images: Bruce Farnsworth (c). 42 Alamy Images: Graphic Science (t). 43 Alamy Images:
Interfoto/Botany (cb). 44–45 Dreamstime.com: Ambience (Animal silhouettes). 46 Alamy Images: Krys Bailey (c).
47 Alamy Images: Ton Koene/Horizons WWP (cb). 48 Alamy Images: Bob Masters (t). 49 Alamy Images: Frans
Lemmens (t). 51 Corbis: Kevin Schafer (ca). 52 Alamy Images: Ammit (t). 54 Alamy Images: David Wall (c).
55 Alamy Images: ZUMA Press, Inc. (t). 56 Alamy Images: Maxime Dube (b). 57 Alamy Images: Maxime Dube (t).
58 Alamy Images: Maxime Dube (cl).
Jacket images: Front: Corbis: Gyro Photography/Amanaimages (t); Dreamstime.com: Janpietruszka;
Back: Dorling Kindersley: Rough Guides

All other images © Dorling Kindersley
For further information see: www.dkimages.com

Discover more at
www.dk.com

Contents

4 **Day 1** My arrival

12 Things to Bring

14 Map to the Research Station

16 **Day 3** Boa Vista

20 The Story of Yara

22 Amazon Animals

24 **Day 4** The Rio Branco

28 **Day 5** In the Rainforest

32 **Day 6** In the Rainforest

36 Footprints Guide

38 Rainforest Layers

40 **Day 9** Tulu Tuloi Hills

44 Olliztli Board Game

50 **Day 22** Research Station

58 Lost City of Z is Found!

59 Rainforest Explorer Quiz

60 Glossary

61 Index

62 Guide for Parents

Amazonian Blog

Day 1 My arrival

Posted by Zoe Dorado

I am exhausted! But I am also very excited. I have arrived in Boa Vista in Brazil and have met my Uncle Renaldo. We are getting ready to go to Uncle Renaldo's Rainforest Research Station. Uncle Renaldo is studying the animals in northern Brazil. He wants to find out if the number of animals is decreasing because of the loss of rainforest.

4

I am looking forward to helping him with the research.

I landed in Brazil earlier today at the Val de Cans Airport, which is a very busy, modern airport near Belém. The man who checked my passport said the airport has 160 flights every day.

In the new terminal building
I changed my money into
Brazilian Reals. I was fascinated
to see that the banknotes show
rainforest wildlife: the 10 Reals
has a parrot, the 20 Reals has
a monkey and the 50 Reals
has a jaguar. I hope I don't
meet a hungry jaguar!

My journey continued on a small propeller aircraft flying to the Boa Vista Airport. On the flight I read the in-flight magazine. One article was about people cutting down the rainforest. The rainforest around the Amazon River is vast, covering 5,500,000 square kilometres.

However, around 600,000 square kilometres has already been cut down. That is terrible! The animals' homes are being destroyed and their habitats are getting smaller. The land is being used for farming. I suppose the farmers need to live somewhere as well.

Another article was about the strange finds at Kuhikugu. This is a village in the rainforest far to the south of Boa Vista. People there have found the ruins of towns, roads and ditches that are hundreds of years old. Thousands of people must have lived there once. Today the ruins are covered by rainforest. How mysterious!

Uncle Renaldo met me at the Boa
Vista Airport, which is very small.
He took me to a hotel through
the bustling town of Boa Vista.

We ate a dinner of pato no tucupi.
This is pieces of duck cooked with
grated manioc root.

10

Manioc, pronounced man-ee-ok, is a bit like a soft potato and it's a very popular dish here. Uncle says that we'll eat it nearly every day.

I must finish this entry now and upload it to the blog. Then I can go to sleep. I wonder what will happen tomorrow.

Things to Bring

Dear Zoe,
Here is a list of clothes and equipment you will need to buy before you begin the journey to my Research Station. Uncle Rx

1. A canvas hat

Make sure it has a wide brim. This will keep the sun out of your eyes and the rain off your head.

2. Walking boots

We'll be doing a lot of walking so you'll need leather boots that are tough but comfortable. They must lace up above your ankle to give support.

3. Boot nets

These are small net
bags that you'll put
your boots in at night.
This will stop scorpions,
snakes or dangerous
insects getting inside them.

4. Sam Browne belt

This is a wide leather belt
with several metal rings
stitched to it.
You'll clip things such as
a water bottle, knife,
notebook and binoculars
to the rings. You need to
buy those things as well.

Map to the Research Station

Key

 By aeroplane

 By boat

 On foot

------- Route

● Belém City

● Boa Vista village

● Research Station

Here is how to pronounce some of the place names:
  Caracaí [KARA-kie]
  Kuhikugu [KOO-ee-koo-goo]
  Tulu Tuloi [TOO-loo TOO-loy]
  Xeriuini [SHE-ree-oo-eenee]

South America

Brazil

Rio Branco

Rio Negro

Amazon River

Brasilia
(capital of Brazil)

Amazon rainforest

Amazonian Blog
Day 3 Boa Vista
Posted by Zoe Dorado

I have had a busy few days in Boa Vista. I have packed what I will need for the trip in a special rucksack Uncle Renaldo gave me. I am ready to go and I can't wait.

Yesterday Uncle introduced me to his friend Pedro, who is a member of the Yanomani Amazon tribe. Uncle Renaldo says we will all leave very early tomorrow morning.

16

It will be nice and cool then, but it is hot now. The thermometer says the temperature is 38°C, and it's raining very hard.

It rains for about five hours each day. No wonder they call this the 'rainforest'!

We plan to travel down the Rio Branco – that means 'White River' – towards the town of Caracaí. This river is a tributary of the great Amazon River.

This Rio Branco is actually a mud brown colour. It is called the 'White River' because there is a Rio Negro – 'Black River' – that flows to the south and really is black in colour. The Rio Negro looks like strong black tea. Weird!

The Story of Yara
Pedro told me this legend...

Macu, a brave hunter, went fishing. He came back that evening to his village with several fine, big fish. He told his friends that he had met a beautiful young woman. She had been sitting on a rock beside the river combing her hair.

Macu said the woman's name was Yara, and she had helped him catch the fish.

Each day, Macu went fishing and each time he told his friends afterwards that he had met Yara. His friend Rona decided to follow him, as he was fascinated to see the mysterious, beautiful Yara. Rona watched as Macu began fishing and then Yara arrived.

She had fair skin and dark green hair.
Rona realised that Yara was a water spirit.
He was frightened and ran back to the village.
That evening Macu did not return
to the village. He never came back.

Ten years later, Rona
was fishing from his canoe.
He dropped an anchor into
the river. A few minutes later
there was a loud splash.
He saw the beautiful Yara
swimming towards him.

"Please lift your anchor," said
Yara. "It is blocking the door
to my home. I cannot get in
to see my husband Macu and
our five children."

In shock, Rona hastily lifted the
anchor and watched as Yara
dived back under the water.

Amazon Animals

Thousands of different types of animal live in the Amazon rainforest. The rainforest is full of colour, sounds and danger.

1. Amazon ants
There are over 1,000 different types.

2. Scarlet macaw
This is one of the most colourful parrots.

3. Toucan
Its impressive beak is a third of its length.

4. Jaguar
This powerful hunter can climb and swim.

5. Anaconda
This giant snake can grow to 9 m (30 ft).

6. Capybara
This is the world's largest rodent.

7. Blue morpho butterfly
This insect dazzles with a 20 cm (8 in.) wingspan.

8. Peccary
Its tusks rub together to make a chattering noise.

9. Tapir [TAY-peer]
Its snout is like a short elephant's trunk.

10. Hummingbird
Its rapid wingbeat helps it to hover at flowers.

23

Amazonian Blog

Day 4 The Rio Branco

Posted by Zoe Dorado

Zoe here – but only just. What an adventure and a narrow escape! Pedro and I went fishing just now to catch something for lunch. I was sitting on the edge of the canoe with a couple of fish he had caught when a barge went past. The wave from the barge made the canoe rock and I fell into the water. Uncle Renaldo started

24

shouting. Pedro threw a rope
to me and pulled me out
of the river. Pedro looked
frightened. Uncle Renaldo
kept asking if I was safe.
They both looked very worried.

They told me that dangerous piranha live in the Rio Branco. Piranha are fish that live in groups of up to several hundred fish. If they smell blood in the water, they will attack and can kill a person in just a few seconds. How frightening is that? Uncle Renaldo is now frying fish and peas in peanut oil. We will eat this with boiled manioc.

As we travelled along the river,
we passed several villages.

At one village, a crane was lifting
huge blocks of white stone on to
a barge tied to the river bank.

I recognised this as marble, which
is used to make sculptures or for
building. We also saw barges
carrying copper ore. I was
surprised to see cranes and
mines in the rainforest.

Amazonian Blog
Day 5 In the Rainforest
Posted by Zoe Dorado

We are camped beside a small stream in the rainforest. It is raining, again! Uncle Renaldo set up a canvas canopy and lit a fire. We had manioc (of course) with dried peas. I am getting bored with eating manioc – I'd love a burger. We left the canoe at the town of Caracaí, which is much smaller than Boa Vista.

28

We rode on a truck to
the village of Igarape.
The farmers in the village grow
manioc to eat, as well as
soya beans and pineapples
that they sell in Caracaí.

The road is just dirt and gravel.
In places there were deep
holes filled with water and mud.
All the trees had been cut down
along the sides of the road. Other
roads led off into the forest and
I noticed that the trees were
being cut down there as well.
There's no road after Igarape –
only paths through the forest.
We began walking after lunch
and walked until almost night.

I was looking for animals but
I didn't see a single one.

It is very dark here. Even in the
middle of the day, it's gloomy
as the huge leaves and branches
overhead block out nearly all
the sunlight. I could hear animals
calling above me, but I couldn't
see any as they were hidden
by the leaves. Perhaps I will see
something tomorrow. Good night.

Amazonian Blog

Day 6 In the Rainforest

Posted by Zoe Dorado

Wow! Pedro has just shown me some round marks in the soil near our tent. They are the footprints of a jaguar, which came to our camp in the night. This big cat can grow to be 2 metres long and weigh 150 kilograms. I didn't hear anything, but Pedro says you never hear the jaguar. It moves like a shadow and kills silently, biting into

32

a skull with its long teeth. You are dead before you hear it. Pedro laughed when he told me this and saw the fear on my face. Thankfully, jaguars don't attack humans unless threatened, as we are too dangerous.

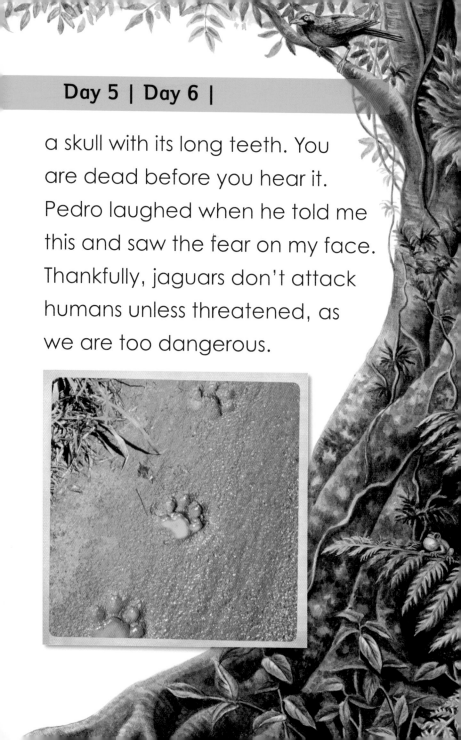

Pedro has pointed to other footprints and told me which animals had made them. Now that I know what to look for, I can see signs of animals everywhere.

I have spotted lots of footprints and even some birds, frogs and insects. Today we will climb up into the hills where the forest becomes less dense. Pedro says that there will be bushes and short trees, as well as the giant rainforest trees. We are near Rio Xeriuini and getting close to Pedro's home, Shadea.

Footprints Guide

for animals in the Amazon rainforest

Capybara

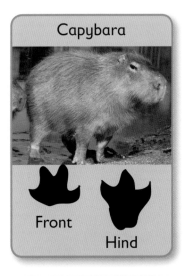

Front

Hind

Armadillo

Front

Hind

Jaguar

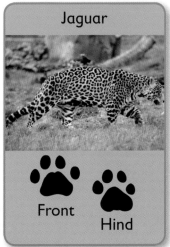

Front

Hind

Black caiman

Front

Hind

Kinkajou

Front   Hind

Tapir

Front   Hind

Ocelot

Front   Hind

Red brocket deer

Front   Hind

37

Rainforest Layers

The rainforest is made up of a number of layers of plant life. Different kinds of animals live in different layers of the rainforest.

Canopy

The most important layer is called the canopy. This is about 30 m (98 ft) above the ground. The branches of the trees form a solid layer of leaves, branches and twigs. Most animals live in this layer. The layer is so thick that it blocks 90% of the light.

Understorey

This is made up of tree trunks and climbing plants. Some birds, lizards and insects live here.

Forest floor

There are a few plants such as ferns or bushes growing here. There is not enough light for much to grow. When a tree dies and falls, sunlight can reach the forest floor. Then hundreds of seeds come to life and grow rapidly. One of them becomes a tall tree that again blocks the light.

Emergent

This is made up of a few very tall trees that reach up to 40 m (130 ft) tall. These tall trees emerge from the canopy.

Amazonian Blog

Day 9 Tulu Tuloi Hills
Posted by Zoe Dorado

For the last three days, I have been living with the Yanomani tribe. It is great. They are very friendly and have wonderful ways of doing things. We even had a feast!
We are in the village where Pedro comes from. The village is made up of a huge wooden house, called shabono. It is shaped like a huge doughnut and its roof is

40

made of dried leaves. About
80 people live inside this shabono.
I am staying in a room with two
girls my own age – Kara and Haxi.

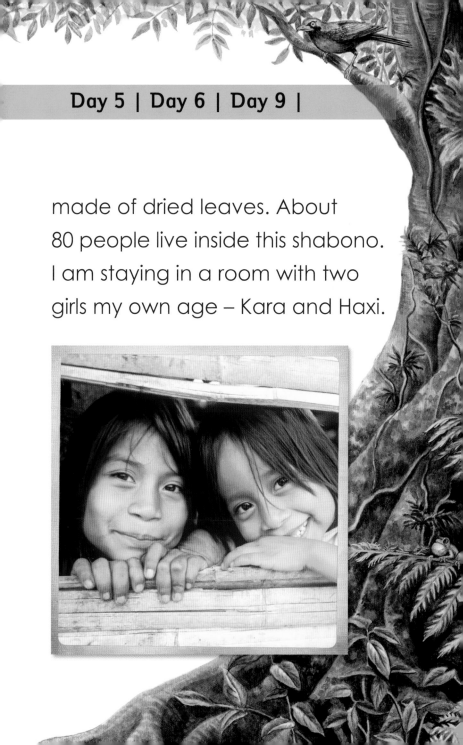

On the first morning, I went out working with Kara and Haxi. We walked to a large mound of hard earth, which was a termite nest. I helped Kara and Haxi to dig out the young termites. They look like fat caterpillars. We ate them fried for lunch and they tasted a bit like hazelnuts.

In the afternoon, we went to the village garden. This is a clearing in the forest surrounded by a wooden fence to keep out deer and other animals. Women grow different types of plants for food. Kara dug up some manioc roots, while Haxi and I picked bananas.

When we finished, we played a game called olliztli.

Olliztli Board Game

You will need:
a copy of the board drawn here,
six red counters and six blue counters
and a die.

1 Each player throws the die.
The player with the highest
number goes first.

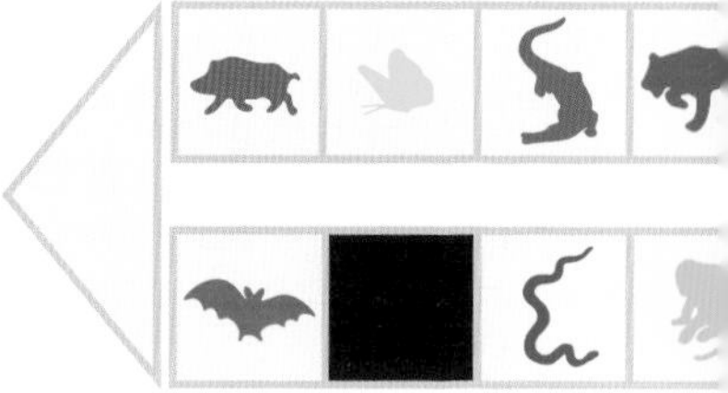

2 The first player puts
her first counter on the
square with the same
colour as her counters.

3 She throws the die
and moves her counter
clockwise the same
number of squares
as the number shown
on the die.

4 The second player
then takes his turn.

5 The players then
take turns to throw
the die. If a 6 is thrown,
a new counter must
be put on to the board.
If a different number
is thrown, the player
may move any of
his/her counters.

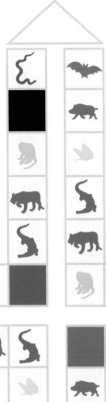

6 A counter cannot land on a square already occupied by another piece.

7 If a counter lands on a black square, the player misses a turn.

8 If no counter can be moved, the player does not move any counters.

9 When a counter has gone right around the course and returns to its starting coloured square, it is removed from the board.

10 The first player to remove all his/her counters from the board is the winner.

45

The men returned from hunting with a capybara and a tapir. There was far too much meat for us all to eat, so people from another village were invited to a big feast the next day.

I helped to wash and peel the manioc roots, which I then grated and mixed with some water to form a paste.

A woman then formed the paste into a flat disc about 30 centimetres across. She dropped it on to a hot stone next to a fire. Within a few minutes, the disc puffed up, looking like a bubbly pancake. I took it off the stone and put it in a basket. We cooked dozens of these pancake things.

The feast was a great success.
A group of men played music
on drums and flutes. Everyone
danced and then feasted.
An old tribesman told us stories
about the past. Then there was
more dancing and more eating
and we went to bed very late.

Tomorrow we must leave the village of Shadea as some people from a nearby tribe are coming to visit. This tribe has never made contact with people from outside the rainforest. They might catch our germs and get sick, or they might think we are invading their land.

Amazonian Blog
Day 22 Research Station
Posted by Zoe Dorado

We reached Uncle Renaldo's
Station ten days ago. It is really
interesting. Uncle Renaldo has
been showing me the work he and
Pedro are doing. They have been
counting how many of each
animal there are. They catch
some animals and weigh, measure
and photograph them before
letting them go. This is an armadillo.

50

But my big news is not about animals. It is about what I found in the rainforest soon after we arrived here. I am thrilled! You will soon see me on television!

Do you remember I told you about the magazine article about Kuhikugu? I found a ditch exactly the same as those in the magazine. I followed the ditch through the rainforest and it formed a square about 200 metres across.

Near the river were the ruins
of a strange structure of stone.
It looked a bit like a dam. I took
photos of the ditches and drew
a sketch map. I also found large
areas of strange black soil.

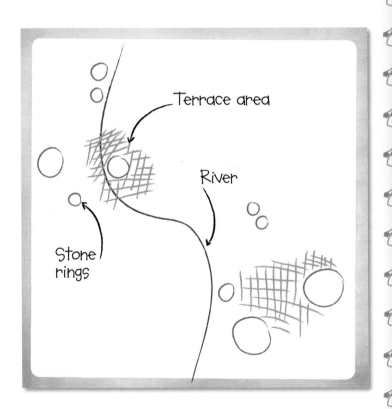

Terrace area

River

Stone
rings

Uncle Renaldo sent my findings over his satellite upload direct to the National Museum of Brazil. Two days later a helicopter arrived.

Professor Gonzales from the
National Museum and a team
of researchers were on board.
They stayed here for several days,
digging holes at the ruins, collecting
things and taking photos. Gonzales
and his assistants found several
other ditches and ruins.

Professor Gonzales says he thinks there was a mighty civilisation in the Amazon rainforest in the past. Great cities and towns once stood on this site and in other places. He thinks over 5,000 people lived here then, but new diseases brought by settlers from Europe wiped out the civilisation.

Professor Gonzales says my finds
are very important. He wants me
to go to the National Museum
in Brasilia to give a talk about
how I found the ruins. Television
cameras will be there so I will
be famous around the world.
I can hardly wait. How exciting!
What a wonderful visit I have
had to the rainforest.

Lost City of Z is Found!

A schoolgirl has found a lost city in the Amazon rainforest. Scientists think the ruins are the Lost City of Z mentioned in old legends.

The ruins found by Zoe Dorado include a dam, a bridge, a fortress and dozens of houses. Only a small part of the site has been explored. Experts think the entire site might include 2,000 houses as well as temples and other buildings.

"This is a major find," said Professor Gonzales of the National Museum of Brazil. "Nobody has ever found such a large ruined city in the rainforest before. We need to go back to the site and study it properly. I shall lead the team and ask Zoe to come with us."

Zoe Dorado, 13, explained how she made her find. "I was helping move some equipment when I saw a ditch. It looked as if it had been made by humans, not by an animal. That is what I first noticed. I came back later to study the ditch. I measured it and took photos that I sent to Professor Gonzales. I did not realise how important the finds were until the Professor told me."

In 1925 the famous British explorer Percy Fawcett vanished without trace in the Amazonian rainforest. He had told friends he was going to look for the Lost City of Z. Nobody knows what happened to Fawcett. It now looks like the lost city has been found.

Rainforest Explorer Quiz

1. What is the name of the banknotes in Brazil?

2. What is the name of the popular soft potato-like food?

3. Which animal has a snout like a short elephant's trunk?

4. Why were Pedro and Uncle Renaldo worried when Zoe fell into the Rio Branco?

5. What is the name of the huge wooden house where all the Yanomani villagers lived?

Answers on page 61.

Glossary

assistant
person who helps
with some work

barge
long, flat-bottomed
boat that carries
loads along a canal

blog
website where
someone
often writes
their thoughts

civilisation
developed
community
of people

habitat
home and
surroundings of
a plant or animal

professor
teacher at a
university or college

rodent
a mammal with
incisor teeth that
keep growing so
it needs to gnaw
constantly

satellite
piece of equipment
that orbits the Earth

terminal
building at an
airport where people
get on and off
aeroplanes

tributary
river that flows
into a main river

Index

Amazon River 8, 18

anaconda 22

armadillo 36, 50

barge 24, 27

Brazilian Reals 7

canopy 28, 38, 39

capybara 22, 36, 46

civilisation 56

dam 53, 58

ditch 52, 53, 55, 58

equipment 12, 58

feast 40, 46, 48

fishing 20, 21, 24

footprints 32, 34, 35, 36

forest floor 38

habitats 9

insects 13, 35, 39

jaguar 7, 22, 32–33, 36

manioc 10, 11, 26, 28, 29, 43, 46

monkey 7

piranha 26

rain 12, 17, 18, 28

rainforest 4, 8–9, 18, 27, 28–39, 49, 51, 52, 56–57, 58

ruins 9, 53, 55, 57, 58

Sam Browne belt 13

tapir 22, 37, 46

termite 42

tributary 18

village 9, 21, 27, 29, 40, 43, 46, 49

wildlife 7

Answers to the Rainforest Explorer Quiz:
1. Brazilian Reals; 2. Manioc; 3. Tapir; 4. Piranha lived in the river; 5. Shabono.

Guide for Parents

DK Reads is a three-level interactive reading adventure series for children, developing the habit of reading widely for both pleasure and information. These chapter books have an exciting main narrative interspersed with a range of reading genres to suit your child's reading ability, as required by the National Curriculum. Each book is designed to develop your child's reading skills, fluency, grammar awareness, and comprehension in order to build confidence and engagement when reading.

Ready for a *Starting to Read Alone* book

YOUR CHILD SHOULD

- be able to read most words without needing to stop and break them down into sound parts.
- read smoothly, in phrases and with expression. By this level, your child will be mostly reading silently.
- self-correct when some word or sentence doesn't sound right.

A VALUABLE AND SHARED READING EXPERIENCE

For some children, text reading, particularly non-fiction, requires much effort but adult participation can make this both fun and easier. So here are a few tips on how to use this book with your child.

TIP 1 Check out the contents together before your child begins:

- invite your child to check the blurb, contents page and layout of the book and comment on it.
- ask your child to make predictions about the story.
- chat about the information your child might want to find out.

TIP 2 Encourage fluent and flexible reading:

- support your child to read in fluent, expressive phrases, making full use of punctuation and thinking about the meaning.

- encourage your child to slow down and check information where appropriate.

TIP 3 Indicators that your child is reading for meaning:

- your child will be responding to the text if he/she is self-correcting and varying his/her voice.

- your child will want to chat about what he/she is reading or is eager to turn the page to find out what will happen next.

TIP 4 Praise, share and chat:

- the factual pages tend to be more difficult than the story pages, and are designed to be shared with your child.

- encourage your child to recall specific details after each chapter.

- provide opportunities for your child to pick out interesting words and discuss what they mean.

- discuss how the author captures the reader's interest, or how effective the non-fiction layouts are.

- ask questions about the text. These help to develop comprehension skills and awareness of the language used.

A FEW ADDITIONAL TIPS

- Read to your child regularly to demonstrate fluency, phrasing and expression; to find out or check information; and for sharing enjoyment.

- Encourage your child to reread favourite texts to increase reading confidence and fluency.

- Check that your child is reading a range of different types, such as poems, jokes and following instructions.

Series consultant **Shirley Bickler** is a longtime advocate of carefully crafted, enthralling texts for young readers. Her LIFT initiative for infant teaching was the model for the National Literacy Strategy Literacy Hour, and she is co-author of *Book Bands for Guided Reading* published by Reading Recovery based at the Institute of Education.

Here are some other
DK Reads you might enjoy.

African Adventure
Experience the trip of a lifetime on an African safari as recorded in Katie's diary. Will she see the Big Five?

The Great Panda Tale
The zoo is getting ready to welcome a new panda baby. Join the excitement as Louise tells of her most amazing summer as a member of the zoo crew.

Battle at the Castle
Through the letters of a squire to his sister, discover life in a medieval castle during peacetime and war. Will the castle fall to the French army or will help come in time?

Shark Reef
Blanche, Ash, Harry and Moby are the sharks who live on the reef. Be entertained by their encounters with the shark visitors that come passing through.

Space Quest: Mission to Mars
Embark with five astronauts on a mission to explore the planets of the solar system. First stop – Mars.

LEGO® Friends: Summer Adventures
Enjoy a summer of fun in Heartlake City with Emma, Mia, Andrea, Stephanie, Olivia and friends.